A Kalmus Classic Edition

Franz

WOHLFAHRT

SIXTY STUDIES

Opus 45

BOOK I (Nos. 1 - 30)

FOR VIOLIN

K 04037

Kalmus

PREFACE

The study of the violin presents certain difficulties for beginners which are frequently the cause of a sudden abatement in the pupil's zeal and ambition, even before he has mastered the first rudiments.

The blame for this is commonly laid on the teacher, who is called incapable or negligent; losing sight of the fact that the pupil began his studies without the slightest notion, not merely of the difficulties to be encountered, but also of the regular and assiduous industry indispensable for surmounting them.

It is important, therefore, to smooth these first asperities by showing their utility and making them agreeable; to this end my Violin Method was published and the present Exercises have been written, which latter may be considered as forming a supplement to the former.

If practised carefully and intelligently, they will serve as a solid foundation for the technique of any player ambitious to become an artist.

Etuden. | Studies.

⊓ Herunterstrich.
V Hinaufstrich.

Die Finger möglichst lange liegen lassen.
Das linke Handgelenk sehr ruhig.

⊓ Down - bow.
V Up - bow.

Hold the fingers down as long as possible.
The left wrist very quiet.

Franz Wohlfahrt. Op. 45, Book I.

Nº 1. Allegro moderato.

BELWIN MILLS PUBLISHING CORP.

PRINTED IN U.S.A.

Auch bei der zweiten, dritten und siebenten Etude benutze man die vor Etude I stehenden Stricharten.

In the second, third and seventh Études the same bowings that were given for the first Étude are to be used.

No. 2. Allegro moderato.

No. 3. Moderato.

No. 4. Allegretto.

No. 5. Moderato.

Nº 6. Moderato.

Nº 7. Allegro moderato.

Nº 8. Largo.

Nº 9. Allegretto.

Genau aufpassen bei Gis auf der D-Saite und bei D auf der A-Saite.

Aufpassen bei D auf der A-Saite und bei As auf der E-Saite.

Pay attention to G♯ on the D-string and to D on the A-string.

Look out for D on the A-string and for A♭ on the E-string.

Nº 10. Moderato.

Nº 11. Moderato.

Nº 12. Allegro.

No. 13. Moderato.

No. 14. Allegro non tanto.

Nº 15. Allegro.

Nº 16. Moderato.

Nº 17. Moderato assai.

Nº 18. Allegro.
mf
f
rit.
a tempo

Bei den letzten 3 Takten behalte man immer dieselbe Strichart bei.

In the last three measures, employ the same bowing without change.

Nº 19. Moderato.

Nº 20. Allegro.

Nº 21. Allegro.

No. 22. Allegro.

No. 23. Moderato.

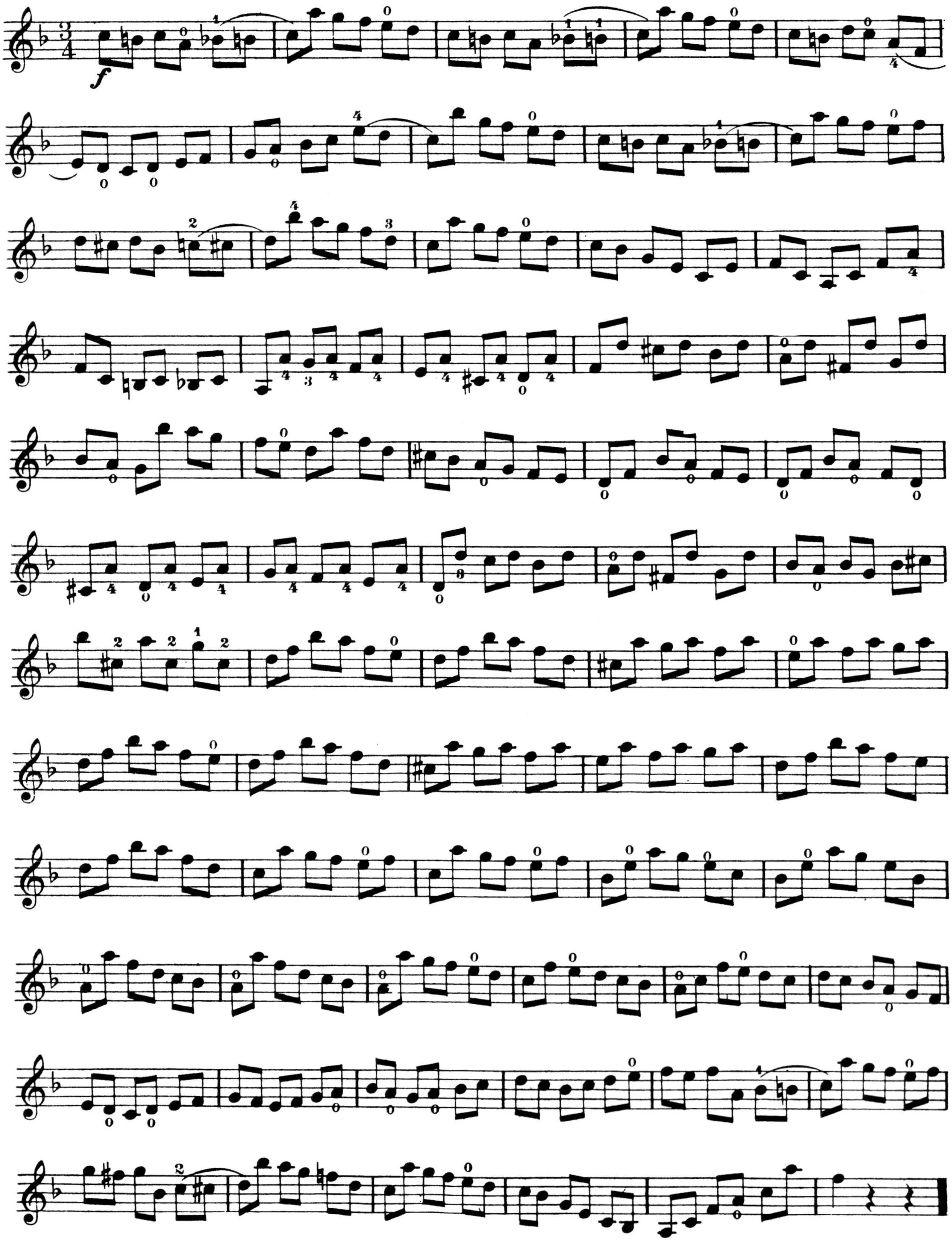

Nº 24. Moderato assai.

Nº 25. Allegro.

No. 26. Allegro.

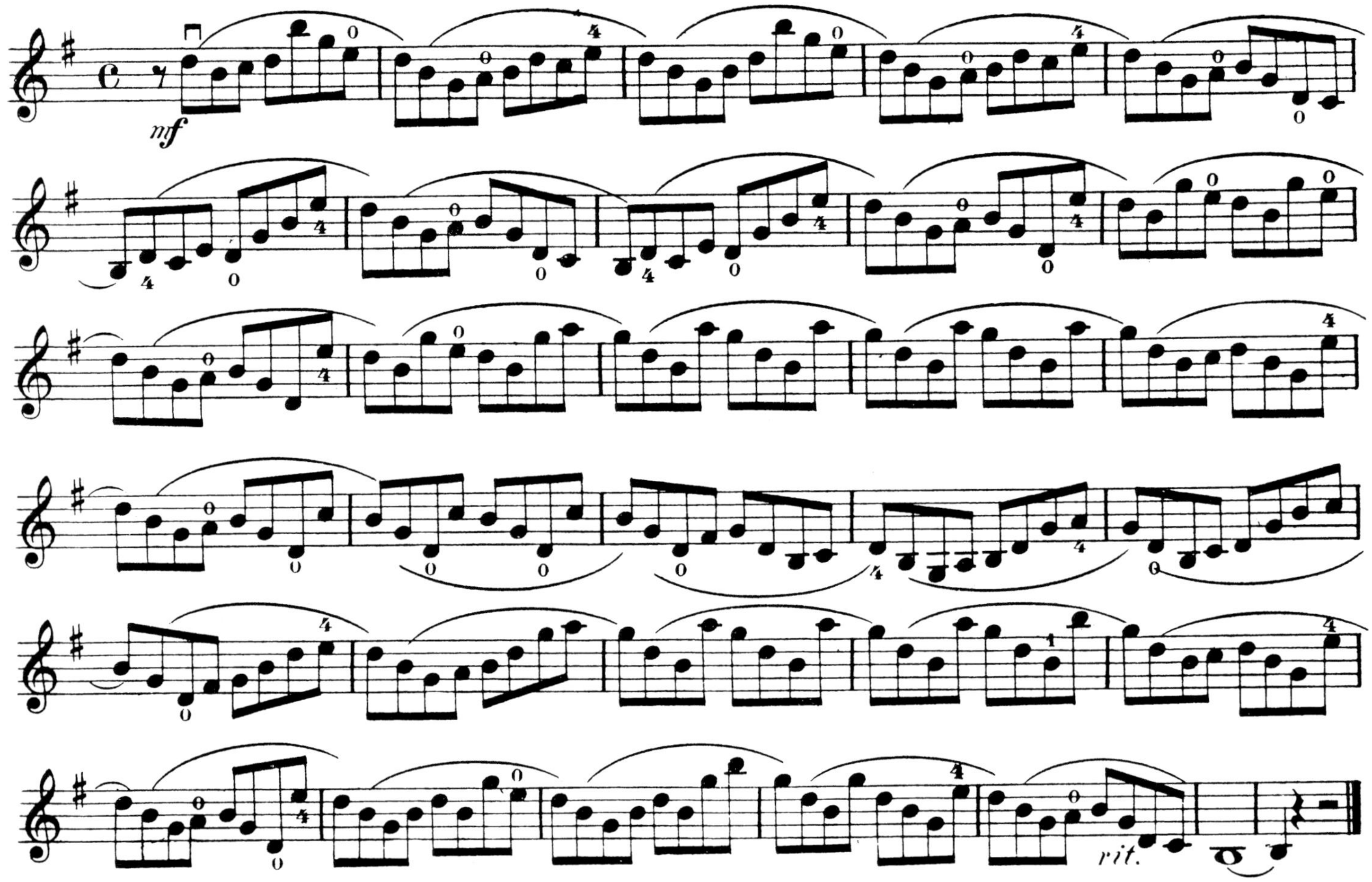

No. 27. Allegro.

Nº 28. Allegretto.

Nº 29. Moderato.

No. 30. Allegro.

Kalmus